The Hunchback of Notre Dame

By Victor Hugo

Retold by Tim Wynne-Jones
Illustrated by Bill Slavin

KPk
Key Porter Kids

Text copyright © 1996 by Tim Wynne-Jones
Illustrations copyright © 1996 by Bill Slavin

Canadian Cataloguing in Publication Data

Wynne-Jones, Tim
      The hunchback of Notre Dame

ISBN 1-55013-773-5

I. Slavin, Bill. II. Hugo, Victor, 1802–1885. Notre-Dame de Paris. III. Title.

PS8595.Y59H85	1996	jC813'.54	C96-930500-1
PZ7.W95Hu	1996		

Key Porter kids
is an imprint of
Key Porter Books Limited
70 The Esplanade
Toronto, Ontario
Canada M5E 1R2

Design: Jean Lightfoot Peters

Printed and bound in Singapore

96 97 98 99 6 5 4 3 2 1

t was the night of the Festival of Fools.

All of Old Paris was crazy with excitement. Crazy to dance in mad costumes around the may pole, to drink and sing around the bonfire in the Place de Grève. And crazy to crown a new King of Fools.

The stage at the Palace of Justice was set for Tragedy, but Clopin the Beggar King had other ideas. "This is no time for actors with long faces!" he heckled. "The crowd is hungry for Comedy!"

Clopin punched a hole through the scenery with his scruffy head. "Who can pull the funniest face? Line up! Line up!"

What an odd cavalcade trooped onto the stage! Then, suddenly, through the hole appeared a face that brought a gasp from the crowd.

"Ahhh!"

It was like a face that had been smashed into a thousand pieces and stitched back together all wrong. Quasimodo the hunchback. Quasimodo the bellringer at the cathedral of Notre Dame.

"Crown him!" clamored the crowd.

How proud Quasimodo was in his cardboard tiara, his tinsel-covered robes, holding the gilded wooden crosier they gave him.

"He's as wicked as he is ugly," yelled someone.

"A Cyclops."

"The devil's handiwork."

But Quasimodo heard only the muffled roar of their applause. He was deaf. The bells of the church had made him that way.

"To the Place de Grève!" cried Clopin. "La Esmeralda waits to dance before her king."

Onto a brightly colored litter Quasimodo leapt. For though his body was as heavy as a bear's and hideously deformed, he was as agile as a lizard.

◆ ◆ ◆

Through the streets the ragged parade bore the King of Fools until, at last, they reached the bonfire at the Place de Grève. The crowd parted and there danced Esmeralda the gypsy girl. A nymph, a goddess. Her streaming black hair jingled with brass coins. A beautiful white goat, its hooves and horns painted gold, pranced around her. Oh, how Quasimodo's heart clattered in his swollen chest to see her dance.

"Look what we've brought you, Esmeralda."

She took one look at him and screamed.

Quasimodo's poor heart broke. He covered his face.

"What is all this?" From the shadows stepped Dom Frollo, the archdeacon of Notre Dame. In his grave presence, a hush fell over the revelers.

Quasimodo leapt down from his litter and groveled at Dom Frollo's feet. It was Dom Frollo who had taken him in when he was a foundling, and Dom Frollo who let him live in the bell tower. He was the archdeacon's faithful dogsbody. Now his master snatched the crosier from Quasimodo's hand and broke it across his knee. He spoke to the hunchback in angry sign language.

"You should know better than to mix with this rabble!" he scolded. But Dom Frollo's eyes looked only upon the beautiful Esmeralda, who cowered under his piercing gaze.

Suddenly, she felt her hair grasped from behind.

"Curse you, daughter of Egypt!"

Esmeralda pulled herself free. A crone's hands clutched at her from between the bars of a low window.

"What have you done with my daughter, gypsy-thief? What have you done with my little Agnes?"

"I have done nothing," gasped Esmeralda. She clutched the charm she kept in a small silken bag on a gold necklace.

"Don't mind her," said a friendly voice. It was Clopin. He helped Esmeralda to her feet. "Sister Gudule has holed herself up in this cell, a prisoner of her sad memories. She does nothing but pray for her lost baby and rave against those who are free."

The half-mad crone returned to her prayers, while the earnest archdeacon led Quasimodo away by the ear.

The crowd grew restless

"We may have lost our King of Fools," said Clopin, "but the night is still young." He handed the gypsy girl her tambourine. "Dance for us, child," he said. The crowd roared their approval.

And so Esmeralda danced.

She danced late into the night.

◆ ◆ ◆

Old Paris slept wreathed in fog. Every street was a jumblement of cold and grasping shadows. Esmeralda stumbled toward her humble home alarmed by every creaking gate and shutter, by every prowling cat. Djali the goat bleated nervously.

"What is it, little friend?"

The hunchback. "Come," he mumbled. "My master bids you come." Quasimodo laid his huge hand on her arm.

"Help!" shouted Esmeralda. "Help!"

"Please don't do that," pleaded Quasimodo.

Her screams alerted the captain of the guards, who charged to the rescue.

"Let her go, you demon!" cried the captain, sweeping Esmeralda onto his horse. Quasimodo grabbed for her, but the captain beat him off. Then his foot soldiers arrived. Quasimodo was surrounded, seized, and bound. He roared at his captors and foamed at the mouth, while the captain whisked Esmeralda away.

"Captain Phoebus de Châteaupers at your service," he said, stroking his mustache.

What dash! What eyes! What arms! Esmeralda was dazzled.

"Captain Phoebus," she said. "Thank you, thank you." She slid down from his horse and, calling Djali to her, ran off home, hearing nothing any longer but the beating of her own heart.

The Court of Miracles. That was Esmeralda's home. She had no other. This was the kingdom of Clopin the Beggar King. A dingy and dilapidated dominion. A secret city of thieves and scoundrels, of gamins and swindlers. A refuge for the cast-off and forgotten, fugitives from the harsh laws of Old Paris. The Court of Miracles had its own set of laws and Clopin was the one who made them. But he was like a father to Esmeralda. She had no other.

◆ ◆ ◆

"Ah, Phoebus," said her friend, the poet Gringoire. "That is what the ancient people called the sun-god."

So that night Esmeralda dreamt of her sun-god Phoebus, the dazzling Captain Phoebus of the guard.

◆ ◆ ◆

Quasimodo had no one to stand beside him at his trial the next morning.

"I was just doing what I was told," he bawled at the judge. But the judge was as deaf as Quasimodo. The court had made him that way.

So the hunchback was dragged off to the pillory at the Place de Grève. In the square where only the night before he had been crowned a king, he now was to be flogged for his sins.

"What a marvelous piece of architecture," said the torturer when the hunchback was chained at his feet. "With a dome for a back and twisted columns for legs."

Then the thin lashes of his whip whistled sharply through the air and cracked against the hunchback's fleshy dome, again and again.

Where was his master? wondered the hunchback. Why did Dom Frollo not come for him?

Suddenly, someone mounted the steps of the pillory. Quasimodo swung his great head to see who it might be. Esmeralda. With water. Ashamed of what he had done to her he cringed, refused her kindness, but she prevailed. No drink had ever tasted so sweet.

"She gave me water," muttered Quasimodo when Esmeralda had gone and he was released at last. He peered down into Gudule's dim chamber. She was kneeling before a single, dainty shoe with satin laces—all she had left of her stolen child. "She gave me water," said Quasimodo. But Gudule was lost in prayer.

Quasimodo climbed up to his bell tower high above the city. He should never have left Notre Dame. It was his egg, his nest, his country. His whole universe. The marble knights and saints did not laugh at him. The gargoyles were his brothers; he could talk to them. And the bells—ah, the bells were his sisters. The church was his sanctuary. The cruel world with its cruel laws could not get at him here.

Meanwhile, in a dark and secret office, Dom Frollo tried in vain to concentrate on his studies. But he was tormented. Down in the square far below his window, Esmeralda danced again. How she mesmerized him. How he longed for her. But his sharp eyes recognized amongst her admirers the one for whom she danced, his armor glittering in the sun. The young and carefree Captain Phoebus.

Esmeralda was in love. Phoebus recognized the signs. And since there were no wars to fight that evening, no riots to quell, a lovely girl made for a pleasant distraction.

Would she walk awhile?

Her smile told him she would walk to the very end of the world for him. He had a closer destination in mind, a secluded tavern, Le Pomme d'Eve.

It grew dark as they walked, his arm around her slender waist. They stopped on the Pont-St. Michel to look at the moonlight reflected in the river Seine.

All at once, a figure in a dark cloak was upon them. Before Phoebus could turn or draw his sword, the assailant had stabbed him and run off into the night.

Horrified, Esmeralda pulled the knife from her beloved's back. "Murderer!" shouted a voice from a lighted window above.

There were many stern faces in the Palace of Justice, and they all looked down upon Esmeralda without a trace of charity.

"The brazen witch. I saw her," claimed the eyewitness. "She stood there clutching the murder weapon in her hand."

Esmeralda shook her head in weary defeat. "No, no, you have it all wrong," she pleaded. "Phoebus was like the sun to me. Better I should have died myself."

"All in good time," said the presiding magistrate.

"Hang her," cried a voice from the gallery. "Hang the gypsy-witch."

In a dungeon as cold as death, Esmeralda lay on a bed of straw,
too numb to sleep, too weak to bother with the crust of stale bread
that was her ration of food. Water dripped from the ceiling and
oozed from the stone walls.

She heard a creaking sound above her, looked up to see a light.
Through a trap door, a cloaked figure with a lantern descended a
flight of stairs carved into the wall. Dom Frollo.

"Do not cringe from me," he said.

Esmeralda stared into his dreadful eyes. "It was you who
killed my Phoebus."

His eyes gave him away. "I did it for love of you," he said. "You
cannot imagine how I suffer. You are in a dungeon—well, so am I.
There is a dungeon inside me. I too am blinded by the darkness
there." He reached out for her. "Only you can save me. Say you'll
be mine, and you are free."

Esmeralda recoiled from his icy hand.

Frollo raged. "Even now they are building a scaffold for you. I
am your last chance."

"Monster!" cried Esmeralda, shoving him away.

◆ ◆ ◆

Day, night—it was all the same. Without the sun, Esmeralda lost all sense of time. But the guards came for her at last. Wearing only her shift, she was to be taken to the cathedral steps to do public penance for her crime, then on to the gallows.

She stood before the great doors of Notre Dame, her head bowed, her hands desperately clutching the charm around her neck though she no longer believed it had any power to protect her. The mighty doors creaked open and a procession of holy men approached her. They were led by Dom Frollo, the wicked archdeacon, chanting loudest of all.

But someone was watching from above. Suddenly, there was a commotion amongst the spectators. A gasp of surprise.

The hunchback.

He swung down on a rope into the courtyard. Guards rushed at him, but he scattered them like bowling pins and took Esmeralda in his arms as gently as a doll.

"Sanctuary!" he bellowed from the doorway of the cathedral. "Sanctuary!"

No one could harm her now. For the church was a place of refuge.

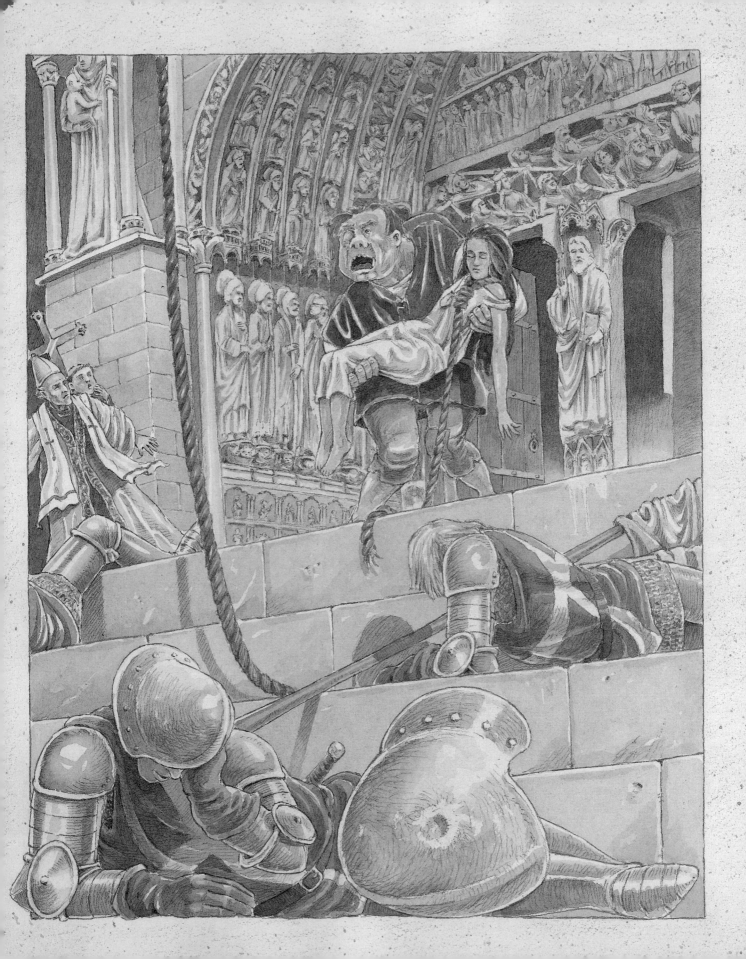

◆ ◆ ◆

How sweetly Quasimodo cared for Esmeralda. He made her a bed in a tiny room in the bell tower, brought her a novice's habit to wear, and gave her flowers from the cloister gardens to brighten her simple cell. He brought her food and wine but would not stay while she ate. "Don't want to spoil your appetite," he said.

At night he slept across the doorway to her room so that no one might disturb her sleep. No one.

He showed her all of his high kingdom. He rang for her the largest bell, the one he called Marie. She smiled for him, so thankful to be alive. But she was not free. For all his kindness, Quasimodo was only another jailkeeper and Notre Dame another jail.

Thoughts of Phoebus filled her aching heart. It was not enough to be loved. How she longed for someone she could love in return.

◆ ◆ ◆

"The sanctuary of the church won't hold off the king's men for long," shouted Clopin. "We must get there first and rescue Esmeralda."

There wasn't a soul in the Court of Miracles who did not agree.

"She is our comrade," cried the poet Gringoire. "It is time to take the law into our own hands."

"To arms!" the grim crowd chanted.

"To Notre Dame!" cried Clopin.

Quasimodo had given Esmeralda a whistle that even he could hear, it was so high-pitched. He awoke one night to the sound of her calling him.

"What is it?" he asked.

She led him to the parapet overlooking the great doors of the cathedral. The courtyard was alive with flaming torches. Quasimodo could see a thousand men and women armed with pitchforks, sickles, pruning hooks, hammers, and crowbars. It was a frightful troop, an army in rags charging the cathedral.

"Who are they?" cried Esmeralda. "What do they want?"

"I will protect you," said Quasimodo.

"Take that!"
he bellowed, heaving
a mighty oak beam over
the balustrade. He roared with
laughter as it fell on the rabble below. He
hurled huge stones down on the ragged army, which
scattered in disarray.

Construction workers had been
fixing the cathedral's roof and had left behind
great vats of molten lead. Lighting fires beneath
the kettles, Quasimodo soon had the metal
bubbling. He tipped the caldrons and watched the
scalding liquid splash across the roofing and out the
grotesque mouths of the drainpipes.

He could not hear the screams from below, but he could see
the strewn bodies, the crowd running in fear.

"You will not get her!" he shouted, dancing around on the
balustrade, making fists at the mob, pulling his tongue.
"Quasimodo will keep her safe!"

But even as he spoke, Esmeralda's shrill whistle came to him once more. Her room was empty. Hearing the whistle again, he followed the sound until he caught sight of her at last, in the grasp of a man in a black cape. He knew only too well who it was.

"Out of my way," Dom Frollo demanded, his voice pitched high, crazy with longing. But Quasimodo was deaf to his command.

"You are not my master anymore," he said.

Wresting Esmeralda from Frollo's clutches, he turned sadly away. And Dom Frollo attacked. A huge slab of stone came down on Quasimodo's back. He stumbled, regaining his balance just as Frollo came at him again, another stone raised above his head. Quasimodo hurled him back against the parapet. With the stone still in his hands, Frollo went crashing over the balustrade to his death.

◆ ◆ ◆

The king's cavalry arrived in the square below. A horrible battle took place by the light of torches. Quasimodo watched in silence, feeling Esmeralda's hand dab at the wounds on his bleeding back. How could he keep her safe in such a cruel world? Was there no refuge?

Weak with fear, she leaned against his side. He held her up, helped her back toward her room. Then something caught his one good eye. He stopped to pick it up. Her charm. Dom Frollo had torn it from her neck, torn the silk bag. When Quasimodo handed it to her, the bag came apart in his thick fingers. He gasped.

"What is it, Quasimodo?"

He was struggling now, struggling with an idea. Then, with a shock, Esmeralda saw a grin fight its way through the anguish on his twisted face.

"This is a miracle," he said.

"Come with me."

He led her down through the darkness of the cathedral. Down spiral stairways and echoing corridors. Down, down through the moonlit gardens where he had picked her flowers, and out a secret low gate into the city.

He led her away from the violent confrontation of forces beyond his understanding or control, down back alleys where Old Paris slept in uneasy peace.

Finally they arrived at the Place de Grève. Esmeralda had first come willingly; now she tugged nervously at his hand.

"No," she said. "Where are you taking me?"

"Trust me," he begged.

He led her across the square, past the pillory where he had been tortured, past the gallows, strung and waiting three days now for its next victim.

Dawn was touching the sky. There was not much time. Soon
the king's men would be combing the streets for Esmeralda.
Quickly Quasimodo led her to the cell where sister Gudule lived.
"Trust me," Quasimodo implored.
He rattled Gudule's cell window.

The crone came immediately, as if she had not been asleep. She made a wicked face, but before she could speak Quasimodo thrust the tiny satin bag before her eyes. Gudule took it and withdrew from its torn side a satin lace, a child's shoe.

"Oh please, that's mine," Esmeralda pleaded. "The woman who cared for me made the purse to hold it so I would never lose it."

Without a word, Gudule brought her the other shoe, its twin, the one she had worshipped so long in her lonely room.

"You!" said Gudule. "You are my Agnes."

There was much weeping and embracing. But the reunion of the mother and child was cut short by the sound of soldiers approaching.

"You are not safe here," said Quasimodo.

Gudule left her cell—the door had never been locked. "I have a few coins people threw to me out of charity for my suffering. Enough to pay a boat man to take us across the Seine. We will return to Reims. I still have a home there."

Everything was happening so quickly. In her astonishment, Esmeralda hardly remembered to wave good-bye to Quasimodo. They were well out on the river when she thought to blow him a kiss. He did not know to catch it. There had been no kisses in his life.

◆ ◆ ◆

And so, his brief, exquisite happiness over, Quasimodo returned to the only mother he knew—Notre Dame. He rang the bells, his beautiful sad sisters, waking all of Paris to the bloody remains of the battle that had been fought at the cathedral doors.

Then he wandered out onto the parapet, where the marble kings and saints did not laugh at him and the gargoyles were his brothers. He said to them what was in his poor, foolish heart.

"Would to God I were made of stone."

THE END